W9-BBX-435

Thomas THE Tank Engine Storybook

Based on the Railway Series by the Rev. W. Awdry

RANDOM HOUSE 🏠 NEW YORK

First American Edition 1993.
Copyright © by William Heinemann Ltd. 1992. Photographs © by Britt Allcroft
(Thomas) Ltd. 1991. All rights reserved under International and Pan-American
Copyright Conventions. Published in the United States by Random House, Inc., New
York. Originally published in Great Britain by William Heinemann Ltd., London. All
publishing rights: William Heinemann Ltd., London. All television and merchandising
rights licensed by William Heinemann Ltd. to Britt Allcroft (Thomas) Ltd. exclusively,
worldwide.

Library of Congress Cataloging-in-Publication Data
Awdry, W. Thomas the Tank Engine storybook.—1st American ed.
p. cm. "Based on the railway series by the Rev. W. Awdry." "Photographs by David
Mitton and Terry Permane for Britt Allcroft's production of Thomas the Tank Engine
and friends"—T. p. verso.
Contents: All about Thomas and his friends—Thomas, Percy, and the dragon—Trust
Thomas—Donald's duck—Edward, Trevor, and the really useful party—A scarf for
Percy—The trouble with mud—No joke for James—Henry's forest—Diesel does it
again—Time for trouble. ISBN 0-679-84465-1
[1. Railroads—Trains—Fiction.] I. Mitton, David, ill. II. Permane, Terry, ill. III.
Awdry, W. Railway series. IV. Title.
PZ7.A9613The 1993 [E]—dc20 92-35915

Manufactured in Hong Kong 10 9 8 7 6 5 4 3 2 1
Random House, Inc. New York, Toronto, London, Sydney, Auckland
Photographs by David Mitton and Terry Permane
for Britt Allcroft's production of
Thomas the Tank Engine and Friends

CONTENTS

ALL ABOUT THOMAS AND HIS FRIENDS

THOMAS THE TANK ENGINE

Thomas, an 0–6–0 tank engine, first came to Sodor on loan from a line in the South of England. The Fat Controller took a special interest in Thomas, and once he had proved himself to be a really useful engine he gave him a branch line of his own. Thomas has worked there happily ever since. His journey runs from Tidmouth to Ffarquhar, where he lives. He has two coaches called Annie and Clarabel.

HENRY THE GREEN ENGINE

The Fat Controller was angry with Henry when he first arrived. It wasn't poor Henry's fault – he couldn't make enough steam because his firebox was too small. Then Henry had an accident when he was pulling The Flying Kipper, and the Fat Controller sent him to Crewe to be rebuilt. He came back with a bigger firebox and a new shape and now enjoys his work. He is based at Tidmouth with Gordon. He is a 4–6–0 engine.

GORDON THE BIG ENGINE

Gordon, a 4–6–2 engine, was built at Doncaster on the other railway as a test engine for a class of which The Flying Scotsman is the only one left. Gordon is a boastful engine, but he works well and the Fat Controller has been heard to remark that he wishes he had two of him. But he is careful not to let Gordon hear him say it!

JAMES THE RED ENGINE

James is a 2–6–0 mixed traffic engine. He can pull trucks or coaches. He came to the Island of Sodor as an 0–6–0, but the Fat Controller had another pair of wheels added in front and replaced his wooden brake-blocks which caught fire on Gordon's Hill when James first arrived. James lives at Tidmouth. He is inclined to grumble but has many times proved himself to be a valuable member of the engine fleet.

EDWARD THE BLUE ENGINE

Edward, a 4–4–0 engine, has been on the island almost as long as Thomas. First he worked at Wellsworth and then at Vicarstown. The Fat Controller brought him back to Wellsworth and put him in charge of the branch line from there to Brendam. Edward works this line with the help of the other engines.

BERTIE

Bertie the bus came to the Island of Sodor soon after Thomas was given his branch line. Like Thomas, he lives at Ffarquhar. Once he rescued Thomas's passengers when he got stuck in a snowdrift. He also had a race with Thomas, though Thomas won. Now they keep each other well supplied with passengers and are the best of friends.

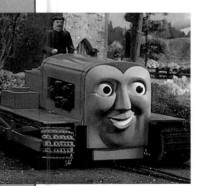

TERENCE

Terence is a tractor with caterpillar tracks. He lives on a farm near Ffarquhar. His special tracks make him a useful friend to have around as Thomas found out soon after meeting him – just the thing for pulling a stuck engine out of a snowdrift.

HAROLD

Harold is a helicopter who lives at Dryaw Airfield near Thomas's branch line. Percy was the first of the Fat Controller's engines to meet him. Percy thought Harold was noisy and Harold kept boasting about how up-to-date he was. Percy challenged him to a race and won, but Harold proved just how useful he was later by parachuting hot drinks to Percy's passengers when he was stuck in a flood. Now they are firm friends.

Sir Topham Hatt

Many years ago Sir Topham Hatt went to work on the Island of Sodor as an engineer to the company that was building a railway there. He was eventually made a director of the line he helped to build. Now he is the chairman.

Percy the Small Engine

No one, not even Sir Topham Hatt, knows where Percy really came from. He's an 0–4–0 saddle-tank engine who has spent much of his time on Sodor keeping Henry and Gordon in their places. Percy has worked hard and Sir Topham Hatt rewarded him by asking him to help with the building of the new harbor at Knapford. Now Percy helps Thomas with the goods traffic on the branch line and in the yard at Ffarquhar.

Toby the Tram Engine

Toby, an 0–6–0 tank engine, was built for work in harbors and on roadside tramways, which accounts for his unusual shape, his side plates and cowcatchers. He keeps the roadside tramway running properly and helps Percy with goods trains too. He has a coach called Henrietta.

Duck

Duck is an 0–6–0 pannier tank Western engine. Duck is his nickname—his proper name is Montague, but he prefers Duck. Sir Thomas Hatt put him in charge of the branch line to Arlsburgh, which he runs with Oliver, another Western engine.

MAVIS

Mavis belongs to the Ffarquhar Quarry Company. She was bought to switch the sidings and was unreliable at first, but after she had helped to save Toby from his tightrope, Sir Topham Hatt and the Quarry Manager decided to give her a chance and allowed her to go down the tramway to Ffarquhar Yard. Now she has become quite useful, and she and Toby work the tramway very efficiently between them.

DIESEL

Diesel is a standard Class 08 shunter from the mainland. He came to the shed "on trial," but he quickly upset the other engines and was sent away in disgrace. Later on, when an emergency arose and Sir Topham Hatt sent for a spare engine, he was not pleased when Diesel was the only one available. But Diesel's behavior improved slightly on this visit, and the bad feeling against him is now less strong than it was.

BILL AND BEN

Bill and Ben are identical twins. They are 0–4–0 saddle-tank engines and belong to the Sodor China Clay Company. They work between the china clay pits and the harbor at Brendam. Edward keeps them in order, and the diesel Boco soon learned their ways as well. Then Boco was able to help when Gordon was sent down the wrong line by mistake!

TREVOR

Trevor is a traction engine. He was sent to the scrapyard because he was thought to be too old to work anymore. This was where Edward met him. Edward persuaded the Vicar of Wellsworth to buy Trevor, and he now lives in the vicarage orchard. He saws logs in winter and gives rides to children at garden parties in the summer.

THOMAS, PERCY, AND THE DRAGON

Thomas and Percy are good friends, but sometimes Percy teases Thomas about being frightened, and he doesn't like that at all.

One evening he was dozing happily, but Percy wanted to talk.

"Wake up, Thomas. Are you dreaming about the time you thought I was a ghost?"

"Certainly not! Anyway, I was only pretending to be scared. I knew it was you really."

Percy went on teasing him.

"I hope the guard leaves the light on for you tonight."

"Why?" asked Thomas. "I quite like the dark."

"Oh really," exclaimed Percy. "I am surprised. I'd always thought you were afraid of the dark—I wonder why!"

Thomas decided to say nothing and went to sleep instead.

Next day, Sir Topham Hatt came to see him.

"I would like you to go to the harbor tonight. You have to collect something rather unusual."

"What sort of something?" asked Thomas.

"Wait and see," replied Sir Topham Hatt.

Meanwhile, Percy was moving freight cars into a siding.

Henry arrived with his goods train. The signalman changed the switches and Percy waited on the siding until Henry had steamed by.

Then there was trouble.

"The switches are jammed," called the signalman. "I can't switch them back for Percy. The workmen will have to mend them in the morning. It's too late now."

"Hmm," said Percy's driver. "I'm sorry, Percy, but you'll have to stay here for the night."

"Where are you going?" asked Percy.

"Home for tea," replied the fireman.

Percy was speechless.

He watched as the other engines went home to the shed.

Nighttime came and Percy began to feel very lonely.

"Oh dear," he murmured. "It's very dark.

"Oh—ooh—what's that!"

It was only an owl, but Percy didn't realize this.

"Oh, I wish Thomas were here too," he sighed.

Thomas was waiting for his mysterious load at the harbor.

Suddenly—there it was!

"Cinders and ashes!" cried Thomas. "It's a dragon!"

"Don't worry," laughed his driver. "This dragon is made of paper. It's for the carnival tomorrow."

Workmen lifted the dragon onto Thomas's low loader and put lights all round it for protection.

Then Thomas set off into the misty night.

Percy was asleep in his siding and had no idea that Thomas was approaching him.

Percy woke up with a start.

"Help!" cried Percy. "I'm not going to open my eyes until my driver comes."

Next morning the switches were mended, and Percy puffed back to the junction.

Gordon was just about to leave with the Express.

"You'll never guess what I saw last night."

Gordon was in no mood for puzzles.

"I'm a busy engine. I don't have time for your games."

"I've seen a huge dragon. It was covered in lights."

Gordon snorted. "You've been in the sun too long. Your dome has cracked."

When the other engines heard the news, they laughed too.

"Look out, Percy," chuckled James, "or the dragon may gobble you up!"

"No one believes me," huffed Percy.

"Maybe I did imagine the dragon after all."

But Percy soon found out that he hadn't.

"Help, save me!" cried Percy.

"It's all right," whistled Thomas, and he explained about the carnival.

"By the way, how was your night out?"

Percy decided to tell Thomas the truth.

"Well, Percy," said Thomas, "maybe we do get scared sometimes, but if we're not afraid to tell each other, then that means we're quite brave too!"

TRUST THOMAS

Thomas the Tank Engine was feeling bright and cheerful. It was a splendid day.

"Good morning," he whistled to some cows, but the cows didn't reply.

"Never mind," said Thomas. "They're busy with their breakfast."

Next he saw Bertie.

"Hello, Bertie. Care for a race today?"

But all Bertie could say was: "Ouch. That's another hole in the road."

"I'm sorry, Bertie," smiled Thomas.

Thomas was still in good spirits when Bertie arrived at the next station.

"Bad luck, Bertie. Now, if you were a steam engine, you would run on a pair of reliable rails."

"Huh," replied Bertie. "The railway was supposed to deliver tar to mend the road two weeks ago. You can't trust a thing that runs on rails."

"I run on rails—you can trust me, Bertie. I'll see if I can find out what's happened." And Thomas puffed away towards the big station.

James was snorting about in the yard.

"It's too bad," he grumbled. "Percy goes to work at the harbor and I do his job—here, there, and everywhere. Take that!"

"Ooh," groaned the freight cars. "Just you wait—we'll show you."

Gordon laughed.

"I'll tell you what, James—if you pretended to be ill *everywhere*, you couldn't shunt freight cars *here* or go to the quarry *there*, could you!"

"What a good idea," agreed James. "Look, here comes Thomas. I'll start pretending now."

Thomas was sorry to see the engines looking miserable.

"Cheer up," he puffed. "It's a beautiful day."

"Yes," grumbled Gordon, "but not for James."

"What's the matter?" asked Thomas.

"He's sick," replied Gordon.

"Yes, he is—I mean, I am," stuttered James. "I don't feel well at all."

"Don't worry," said Thomas kindly. "I'll help out if you're ill."

Gordon and James snickered quietly to each other.

Some of James's cars were coupled behind Thomas, and he steamed away to the quarry.

The cars were still cross.

"We couldn't pay James back for bumping us, so we'll play tricks on Thomas instead. One engine is as good as another."

But Thomas didn't hear them. He collected all the stone from the quarry and set off back to the junction.

Danger lay ahead.

"Now for our plan," giggled the cars. "Go faster, go faster."

They pushed Thomas over the switches.

"Slow down," called Thomas's driver, and applied the brakes.

Poor Thomas stood dazed and surprised in a muddy pond as a toad eyed him suspiciously.

"Bust my buffers," muttered Thomas. "The day started so well, too."

Duck pulled away the cars, and Edward helped Thomas back to the junction.

Suddenly Thomas remembered the missing tar. He told Edward all about it.

"That's strange," said Edward. "A car full of tar has been left at my station. That must be it. Driver will make sure it gets to Bertie now."

Later James spoke to Thomas.

"I'm sorry about your accident," he muttered, "and so is Gordon. We didn't mean to get you into trouble."

"No, indeed," spluttered Gordon. "A mere misunderstanding, Thomas. All's well that ends well."

Just then Bertie arrived. He looked much more cheerful.

"My road's being mended now."

"Oh, I am glad," replied Thomas.

"Thanks for all you did," added Bertie. "Now I know I can trust an engine—especially if his name is Thomas."

Gordon and James puffed silently away to the shed. But Thomas still had company.

"Well, well," he sighed. "What a day for surprises."

The toad, who was looking forward to a ride home, noisily agreed.

DONALD'S DUCK

Duck the Great Western Engine worked hard in the yard at the big station.

Sometimes he pulled coaches, sometimes he pushed freight cars—but whatever the work, Duck got the job done without fuss.

One day Duck was resting in the shed when Sir Topham Hatt arrived.

"Your work in the yard has been good. Would you like to have a branch line for your own?"

"Yes, please, sir," replied Duck.

So Duck took charge of his new branch line.

The responsibility delighted him.

The line runs along the coast by sandy beaches till it meets a port where big ships come in.

Duck enjoyed exploring every curve and corner of the line.

Sea breezes swirled his smoke high into the air, and his green paint glistened in the sunlight.

"This is just like being on holiday," he puffed.

"Well, you know what they say," laughed his driver. "A change is as good as a rest."

Soon Duck was busier than ever.

Sir Topham Hatt was building a new station at the port.

Duck pulled the heavy freight cars of ballast wherever they were needed.

Bertie looked after Duck's passengers, and the other engines helped too, but the work took a long time.

Noise and dust filled the air.

"Don't worry," whistled Toby. "The station's nearly finished."

"And on time, too," said Duck thankfully.

Duck felt his responsibility deeply and talked endlessly about it.

"You don't understand, Donald, how much Sir Topham Hatt relies on me."

"Och, aye," muttered Donald sleepily.

"I'm Great Western and I—"

"Quack, quack, quack."

"What?"

"Ye heard—quack, quack, ye go—sounds like ye'd an egg

laid. Now wheesht and let an engine sleep."

"Quack yourself," said Duck indignantly.

Later he spoke to his driver.

"Donald says I quack as if I'd laid an egg."

"Quack, do you?" pondered his fireman. He whispered something to Duck and his driver.

They were going to play a joke on Donald and pay him back for teasing Duck.

The engines were busy for the rest of the day and nothing more was said.

Not even a quack!

But when at last Donald was asleep, Duck's driver and fireman popped something into his water tank.

Next morning, when Donald stopped for water, he found that he had an unexpected passenger aboard.

A small white duckling popped out of his water tank.

"Na doot who's behind this," laughed Donald.

The duckling was tame. She shared the fireman's sandwiches and rode in the tender. The other engines enjoyed teasing Donald about her.

Presently she grew tired of traveling and hopped off at a station—and there she stayed.

That night, Donald's driver and fireman got busy, and in the morning when Duck's crew arrived to look him over, they laughed and laughed.

"Look, Duck. Look what's under your bunker. It's a nest box with an egg in it."

Donald opened a sleepy eye.

"Well, well, well, ye must have laid it in the night, Duck—all unbeknownst."

Then Duck laughed too.

"You win, Donald. It'd take a clever engine to get the better of you!"

There's a pond near the duckling's station. Here she often

swims and welcomes the trains as they pass by.

    The stationmaster calls her Dilly, but to everyone else she is always Donald's Duck.

EDWARD, TREVOR, AND THE REALLY USEFUL PARTY

Trevor the Traction Engine is old-fashioned, but he doesn't care. He knows that he is really useful—like his friend Edward the Blue Engine.

Early one morning Trevor was chuffing about the vicarage orchard. He had important news for Edward.

"The vicar says that not all children are able to have holidays by the sea, so he's having a garden party to raise money for a seaside trip. I'm going to be the star attraction," chattered Trevor, "giving rides to all the visitors. The vicar is putting up posters all about it."

"I'd like to help too," sighed Edward. "But without my rails I wouldn't be much good at a garden party."

It was a beautiful day, but Edward was worried.

"I wish there were something I could do for the party," he said. "I'd like to be helpful like Trevor."

Edward's driver laughed.

"You're helpful in your own way and that's on the railway!"

Next day it was Trevor's turn to look disappointed. He had bad news.

"The vicar's been so busy that he forgot to put up the posters. Now no one will know about the party."

But Edward had an idea.

"Don't worry," he said. "Everything is going to be all right."

Then he explained to his driver.

"The vicar can paste his posters on my cab and coaches, so wherever I go, they'll go too!"

"Well done, Edward," said his driver. "I'm sure Sir Topham Hatt will agree!"

As indeed he did.

Edward steamed happily through the stations collecting his passengers.

"Look," they said. "The vicar is holding a party—we must go to that!"

Later Trevor was resting in the orchard shed when Bertie rolled by.

"Hello, Trevor. Why are you dozing there like an old stick-in-the-mud?"

"I'm not dozing—I'm resting," replied Trevor.

Then he told Bertie about the vicar's party.

"I'll be there too," boasted Bertie. "I'm not sure people will want to ride on an old traction engine after traveling in a smart red bus like me."

The party day arrived.

It had rained heavily during the night and the orchard ground was soaked.

"Rain and mud won't spoil my day," said Trevor.

"No, indeed," agreed his driver. "We'll stay on the road, then we won't get bogged down."

Trevor was soon busy trundling up and down the quiet country lane, carrying lots of laughing children.

He was just turning a corner when he heard Bertie.

"Hello, old-timer. I'm taking everyone to the party. People have come from all over the island."

Trevor gave Bertie a cheerful whistle and turned back towards the orchard.

Then there was trouble.

"Help, I'm stuck!" shouted Bertie.

His wheels had sunk deep in the orchard mud.

Terence the Tractor arrived just in time.

"I'm the one who has to plow fields," laughed Terence. "We'd better get you out of here."

Using strong ropes, Terence and Trevor pulled Bertie clear of the mud.

"This will teach Bertie a thing or two," Trevor chuffered to himself.

At last Bertie was on the road again.

"Thank you, Trevor. You're not a stick-in-the-mud at all!"

"No," smiled Trevor. "But you were, just for a little while."

That evening the vicar arrived to see Edward and his driver.

"Thanks to your good idea about the posters, hundreds of people paid to come to the party. We've raised lots of money for the children."

Edward was very pleased, and Trevor fell happily asleep thinking of all the children who would now get to the seaside at last.

A Scarf for Percy

It was a cold winter's morning on the Island of Sodor. The wind was bitter and the ground hard with frost.

Thomas and Percy were cold and cross.

"All I want is a warm boiler," huffed Thomas. "Firelighter knows that. He's late."

"He's not late," replied Percy. "This weather woke us up early."

Gusts of wind swirled round the shed, tossing flakes of snow toward Thomas. Then they swooshed round Percy too.

"Why don't we talk about something else?" shivered Percy.

"Yes," replied Thomas. "Like how silly we'll look when our funnels turn into icicles."

"That's not funny. Maybe we'll stop feeling cold if we talk about warm things—like sunshine and steam."

"And firelighters," muttered Thomas.

"Scarves," continued Percy.

"Scarves," laughed Thomas. "That's what you need, Percy. A woolly scarf round your funnel."

Thomas was only teasing, but Percy thought happily about scarves until the firelighter came.

Sir Topham Hatt was enjoying hot porridge for breakfast.

He was looking forward to taking important visitors on a tour of the railway, and had pressed his special trousers.

"I shall put them in my trunk," Sir Topham Hatt said to his wife, "and change into them just before the photographs are taken."

Then he set off to catch his train.

Percy was now working hard. His fire was burning nicely, and he had plenty of steam, but he still thought about scarves.

He saw them everywhere he went.

"My funnel's cold, my funnel's cold," he puffed. "I want a scarf, I want a scarf."

"Rubbish, Percy," said Henry. "Engines don't wear scarves."

"Engines with proper funnels do," replied Percy. "You've only got a small one."

Before Henry could answer, Percy puffed away.

Henry snorted. He was looking forward to pulling the special train.

It was time for the photographs. Everyone was excited.

Sir Topham Hatt was waiting on the platform for his trousers.

They were in a trunk amongst a big load of baggage. The porters were taking the baggage trolley across the line.

They were walking backwards to see that nothing fell off.

Percy was still being cheeky. His driver always shut off steam just outside the station. Percy wanted to surprise the coaches by coming in as quietly as he could.

But the porters didn't hear him either.

Percy gave them such a fright that boxes and bags burst everywhere.

"Oh!" groaned Percy.

Sticky streams of jam trickled down Percy's face.

A top hat hung on his lamp iron.

Worst of all, a pair of trousers coiled lovingly round his funnel.

Everyone was very angry.

Sir Topham Hatt seized the top hat.

"Mine!" he said. "Percy, look at this!"

"Yes sir. I am sir."

"My best trousers too."

"Yes sir. Please sir."

"We must pay the passengers for their spoiled clothes, and my trousers are ruined. I hope this will teach you not to play tricks with the coaches."

Percy went off to the yard. He felt very silly.

On the way he met James.

"Hello, Percy, so you found a scarf, eh? But legs go in trousers, not funnels!" And he puffed away to tell Henry the news.

That evening Thomas and Percy were resting in the shed. Percy's driver had taken away the trousers and given Percy a good rubdown.

"Firelighter's promised to come early tomorrow," said Thomas.

Henry arrived. He'd enjoyed taking the visitors around and now felt sorry for Percy too.

"Driver says the weather will be warmer tomorrow—you won't need a scarf, Percy."

"Certainly not," replied Percy. "Engines don't need scarves. Engines need warm boilers. Everyone knows that."

THE TROUBLE
WITH MUD

One morning Thomas was being cleaned when Gordon arrived.

Mud had blown all over his smart blue paint.

"Hello, Gordon," called Thomas. "You look as if you've

had a mudbath. Be a sensible engine and have a shower instead."

Gordon snorted.

"I haven't time to dawdle over my appearance like fussy tank engines do."

The wind blew stronger.

"Gordon, slow down," called his driver.

This made Gordon crosser still.

"Now I'll be dirty *and* late, dirty *and* late," he hissed.

At the next station was a sign: "All Trains Must Wash Down Daily."

James had just finished being cleaned.

"Come on, Gordon," said his driver, "you'll feel better too after a good hosedown."

"Paah!" said Gordon, and angrily let off steam.

"You're a very naughty engine," said Gordon's driver. "Now James will need another shower. You'll have to wait your turn till later."

"Good riddance," huffed Gordon. "I'm far too busy to waste time with water."

He finished his journey safely and steamed into the big station.

Sir Topham Hatt was waiting. So were Gordon's coaches and the passengers.

"Goodness gracious," said Sir Topham Hatt. "You can't pull the train. Henry will have to do it. Gordon, you'd better get cleaned straightaway."

Gordon was soon being washed.

"Mind my eyes," he grumbled.

Then he pulled cars for the rest of the day.

"Freight trains, freight trains," he spluttered. He felt his position deeply.

"That's for you—and you—and you."

"Cars will be cars," laughed James.

"They won't with me," snorted Gordon. "I'll teach them."

James got ready to take the Express when Gordon returned.

"Be careful," warned Gordon. "The hills are slippery. You may need help."

"I don't need help on hills," replied James huffily. "Gordon thinks he knows everything."

Earlier a storm had swept Gordon's hill, blowing leaves onto the tracks, which made them slippery. Even though the storm had passed, the hill was still difficult to climb. James knew this.

The signal showed "clear," and James began to go faster.

"I'll do it, I'll do it," he puffed.

Halfway up, he was not so sure.

"I must do it, I must do it." But his wheels slipped on the leaves.

He couldn't pull the train at all.

"Help, help!" whistled James.

His wheels were turning forward, but the heavy coaches

pulled him backward.

The whole train started slipping down the hill.

His driver shut off steam, and put on the brakes. Then, carefully, he stopped the train.

Gordon saw everything.

"Ah well, we live and learn. Never mind, little James, I'm going to push behind."

Clouds of smoke and steam billowed from the snorting engines as they struggled up the hill.

"We can do it," puffed James.

"We *will* do it," puffed Gordon.

At last they reached the top.

"Peep, peep. Thank you. Good-bye," whistled James.

"Poop, poop," answered Gordon. "Good-bye."

That night, Sir Topham Hatt came to see the engines. Gordon was miserable.

"Please, sir," said Thomas. "Can Gordon pull coaches again now?"

"If you understand that having a washdown is essential to every engine, then, yes, Gordon, you may."

"Thank you," grunted Gordon.

"Dirty or clean, I'm a famous machine." But no one heard but him.

NO JOKE FOR JAMES

James is a mixed-traffic engine. He can pull both freight cars and coaches.

He is proud of his smart red paint and so is his driver.

"Everyone says you brighten up their day, James."

One morning James whistled loudly at the other engines:

"Look at me, I am the smartest, most useful engine on the line!"

"Rubbish!" replied Thomas. "We're all useful. Sir Topham Hatt says so, and he's head of the whole railway."

"You know what, James," added Percy.

"What?" replied James.

"You're getting all puffed up!"

James huffed away.

Later he was still boasting.

"I'm the pride of the line."

"I saw you pulling freight cars today," snorted Gordon. "You're only a goods engine!"

"I pull coaches too!"

"Not as much as I do."

"But Sir Topham Hatt has plans for *me*." James was only making this up, but Gordon believed him.

"What plans?"

"Er—wait and see."

"Oh dear," he thought. "Now what'll I do?"

Thomas was shunting shining new coaches.

"Good morning, James."

"Are those coaches for me?" asked James hopefully.

"No. These are for Gordon's Express. I'll fetch your freight cars next."

But James was going to play a trick on the other engines.

"Actually, Thomas, I'm taking the coaches. Sir Topham Hatt asked me to tell you."

"What about the cars?" asked Thomas.

"Er—give them to Gordon," ordered James.

"Come on, Thomas," said his driver. "Orders are orders."

So when James's driver returned, James was coupled to the coaches and he puffed away.

Thomas returned with the freight cars and, a few minutes later, Gordon arrived.

"Where's the Express?"

Thomas told him about James.

"And so here are your cars."

Gordon was very cross and so was his driver.

"Wait till Sir Topham Hatt hears about this!"

Meanwhile, James was enjoying himself enormously.

"What a clever plan, what a clever plan," he chuffed.

Then he saw Sir Topham Hatt.

"Some jokes are funny, but not this one, James. You have caused confusion."

"Yes, sir," said James.

"You will now stay in your shed until you are wanted."

The other engines teased James.

"I wonder who'll be pulling the Express today," said Gordon.

"I expect it'll be you," replied Henry. "James is stuck in the shed for being silly!"

James felt sad.

Next morning, he went back to work.

"Hello," whistled Thomas. "Good to see you out and about again."

"I'm sorry I tricked you," said James. "Are these my cars?"

"Yes," replied Thomas kindly. "They are pleased to have you back."

James set off to the harbor with his train of freight cars.

He bustled about all day, pushing and pulling them into place.

"Time to go home now, James," said his driver at last. "No cars or passengers—just we two."

But his driver was wrong.

"Excuse me," called a man. "I have a meeting with Sir Topham Hatt and I mustn't be late. May I ride back with you?"

"Of course," replied James's driver. Then he whispered to James, "This gentleman is a railway inspector."

James was most impressed.

He steamed along the line as smoothly and quickly as he could.

Sir Topham Hatt was waiting on the platform, and the railway inspector greeted him warmly.

"This clever engine gave me a splendid ride. You must be proud of him."

"Yes, indeed.

"Once again you *are* a Really Useful Engine."

HENRY'S FOREST

Henry the Green Engine has lived on the Island of Sodor for many years. He wouldn't want to be anywhere else.

He likes every part of it, from the fields filled with flowers to the white sandy beaches. But there is one place that Henry always enjoyed visiting more than any other.

His driver knew this too.

"Come on, Henry," he would sometimes say. "We've made good time today. We'll stop for a while by the forest."

Henry loved it here. The forest was full of broad oaks and tall pines.

Henry could remember the day long ago when he and Toby brought some new trees to be planted and Terence and Trevor helped haul them into place.

Now he could see the trees growing amongst the others on the hillside.

Henry always felt better for being here. He couldn't really explain why, but his driver understood.

"It's peaceful," he said to Henry.

But one night, everything changed.

The engines were resting in the shed.

"Listen," said Thomas. "Can you hear a strange whistling sound?"

"It's the wind blowing outside our shed," replied Toby. "But I've never heard it like this before."

"Do you know," added James, "if Gordon wasn't here now, I'd say it was him thundering by with the Express."

All the engines laughed, except Henry.

"I hope the wind won't harm the forest."

By morning, the fierce winds had gone, but the damage was done.

Henry's driver came to see him in the yard.

"Trees have fallen on the line," he said. "We must help clear the tracks."

Donald set off with the breakdown train, and Henry followed.

Trees lay everywhere.

The hillside now looked so bare.

Henry felt sad.

"What will happen to all the animals who live here?" he thought.

When Henry's flat cars were full of logs, he took them to the timber mill, where they would be turned into furniture and other things.

Henry was glad the wood was being put to good use, but he was still sorry to lose part of his forest.

"Oh dear," sighed Toby to Thomas. "I wish there was something we could do to make things better again."

"Yes, indeed," replied Thomas. "But what? We can't mend broken trees!"

"Hello, Toby," said Sir Topham Hatt. "You do look glum."

"I'm sad about the trees," said Toby. "And so is Henry. The forest is a special place to him. Now some of it is gone."

"We'll soon put that right," replied Sir Topham Hatt. "I have an important job for you, Toby. I would like you to take some freight cars to the forest."

When the freight cars arrived, Toby was delighted.

They were full of splendid young trees all ready for planting.

"This is the best job I've ever had," said Toby happily.

When Henry returned, he was most surprised.

There were Terence and Trevor busily helping the workmen clear the torn stumps and branches.

"Look, Henry," called Terence. "We're beginning again—

the hillside will look better than ever before, you'll see."

Now whenever Henry stops by the forest, he can see the new trees growing strong and tall.

Sometimes everywhere is very quiet—and at other times Henry can hear leaves rustling, or a bird's wing brushing the air.

Often he can hear the distant sound of children laughing, and always he is happy here.

DIESEL DOES IT AGAIN

Duck and Percy enjoy their work at the harbor, pulling and pushing cars full of cargo to and from the quay. But one morning the engines were exhausted. The harbor was busier than ever.

Sir Topham Hatt promised that another engine would be found to help them.

"Huh! It's about time," said Percy.

"I ache so much I can hardly get my wheels to move," agreed Duck.

They waited for the engine to arrive.

It came as a shock when he did.

"Good morning," squirmed Diesel in his oily voice.

The two engines had not worked with Diesel for a long time.

"What are you doing here?" gasped Duck.

"Your worthy Top—Sir Topham Hatt sent me. I hope you are pleased to see me again. I am to shunt some dreadfully tiresome cars."

"Shunt where?" said Percy suspiciously.

"Where? Why from here to there," purred Diesel, "and then again from there to here. Easy, isn't it?"

With that, Diesel, as if to make himself quite clear, bumped some cars hard.

"Ooooh!" screamed the cars.

"Grrrrrh," growled Diesel.

Percy and Duck were horrified. They did not trust Diesel at all.

They refused to work and would not leave their shed.

Sir Topham Hatt was enjoying his tea and iced bun when the telephone rang.

"So there's trouble in the harbor yard? I'll be there right away!"

Diesel was working loudly and alone.

Cargo lay on the quay. Ships and passengers were delayed. Everyone was complaining about Sir Topham Hatt's railway.

Percy and Duck were sulking in their shed.

"What's all this?" demanded Sir Topham Hatt.

"We're on strike, sir," said Percy nervously.

"Yes," added Duck. "Beg pardon, sir, but we won't work with Diesel, sir. You said you sent him packing, sir."

"I have to give Diesel a second chance," replied Sir Topham Hatt. "I'm trying to help you by bringing Diesel here. Now you must help me. He was the only engine available."

Percy and Duck went sadly back to work.

Next morning, things were no better. Diesel's driver had not put his brakes on properly and Diesel started to move.

He went bump. Straight into Percy!

"Wake up there, Percy," scowled Diesel, "you have work to do."

He didn't even say he was sorry to Percy.

Later, Diesel bumped the cars so hard that the loads went everywhere.

"What will Sir Topham Hatt say?" gasped Percy.

"He won't like it," said Duck.

"So who's going to tell him, I wonder? Two little goody-

goody tattle-tales like you, I suppose."

Percy and Duck did not want to be "tattle-tales," so they said nothing.

Diesel, thinking he could get away with his bad behavior, was ruder than ever.

Next day he was shunting freight cars full of china clay.

He banged the cars hard into the buffers, but the buffers weren't secure.

The silly cars were sunk.

Sir Topham Hatt heard the news.

The cars were hoisted safely from the sea, but the clay was lost.

Sir Topham Hatt spoke severely to Diesel.

"The harbor master has told me everything. Things worked much better here before you arrived. I shall not be inviting you back.

"Now, Duck and Percy—I hope you won't mind having to handle the work by yourselves again."

"Oh no, sir,—yes, please, sir," replied the engines.

Whistling cheerfully, they puffed back to work while Diesel sulked slowly away.

TIME FOR TROUBLE

The Island of Sodor had many visitors, and Sir Topham Hatt had scheduled more trains.

Gordon, the big engine, had to work harder than ever before.

"Come on," he called to the coaches. "Come on, come on,

come on. The passengers rely on me to be on time."

Whenever Gordon finished one journey, it was time for another to begin.

"Never mind," he puffed. "I like a long run to stretch my wheels."

Even so, Sir Topham Hatt decided that Gordon needed a rest.

"James shall do your work," he said kindly.

James was delighted.

He liked to show off his smart red paint and was determined to be as fast as Gordon.

"You know, little Toby," he boasted, "I'm an important engine; everyone knows it. I'm as regular as clockwork. Never late, always on time. That's me."

"Sez you," replied Toby.

Just then Sir Topham Hatt arrived.

"Your parts are worn, Toby, so you must go to the works to be mended."

"Can I take Henrietta, sir?"

"No. What would the passengers do without her?"

Toby saw Percy by the water tower.

"Don't worry, Toby, I'll take care of Henrietta until you get back."

Soon Toby was out on the main line. He clanked as he trundled slowly along.

He's a little engine with small wheels. His tanks don't hold much water.

He had come a long way and began to feel thirsty.

In the distance was a signal.

"Good," he thought. "There's a station ahead. I can have a nice drink and a rest until James has passed."

Toby was enjoying his drink when the signalman came up. He had never seen Toby before. Toby's driver tried to explain, but the new signalman wouldn't listen.

"We must clear the line for James with the Express. You'll have to get more water at the next station."

Hurrying used a lot of water, and his tanks were soon empty.

Poor Toby was out of steam and stranded on the Main Line!

"We must warn James," said the fireman.

Then he saw Percy and Henrietta.

"Please, take me back to the station. It's an emergency."

Henrietta hated leaving Toby.

"Never mind," said Percy, "you're taking the fireman to warn James, that's a big help."

Henrietta felt much better.

James was fuming when he heard the news.

"I'm going to be late."

"My fault," said the signalman, "I didn't understand about Toby."

"Now, James," said his driver, "you'll have to push Toby."

"What, me!" snorted James. "Me push Toby and pull my train too?"

Grumbling dreadfully, James set off to find Toby.

He came up behind Toby and gave him a bump.

"Get on, you."

James had to work very hard.

When he reached the works station, he felt exhausted.

Some children were on the platform.

"Coo, the Express is late and it's got two engines. I think James couldn't pull it on his own, so Toby had to help him."

"Never mind, James," whispered Toby. "They're only joking."

"Hah," said James.

Toby just smiled.

THE PARTS OF THOMAS THE TANK ENGINE

1	COAL BUNKER	10	COUPLING HOOD
2	CAB	11	BRAKE PIPE
3	WATER TANK	12	LAMP BRACKET
4	WHEEL	13	FILLER CAP
5	COUNTERWEIGHT	14	SMOKESTACK
6	COUPLING ROD	15	BOILER BAND
7	SPLASHER	16	DOME
8	VALENCE	17	SPECTACLE WINDOW
9	BUFFER	18	SAFETY VALVE